*For my Clementine -*
*May your dreams be your guideposts,*
*and love, your compass.*
*-T.H.*

Books may be purchased in quantity and/or special sales by contacting the publisher,
Downtown & Brown Ventures LLC, at sales@downtownandbrown.com.

Published by: Downtown & Brown Ventures LLC

Library of Congress Control Number: 2016910358

ISBN: 978-0-997739-1-0-7

10 9 8 7 6 5 4 3 2 1

First Edition First Printing
Printed and Bound in China

Captain Pirate hadn't yet found the Hidden Treasure.

Giant Dinosaur hadn't yet stomped through the Great Divide.

And when Buzzy yelled, the Moon shook.
Quite powerfully! Moon Man nearly fell over!

Moon Man stopped building his Moon Base.

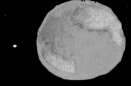

"Be careful!" said Moon Man, quite concernedly. And then Moon Man asked, "What's this all about, Buzzy?"

"I don't want to go to sleep, Moon Man," said Buzzy.

"But Buzzy," said Moon Man, "how will we finish building the Moon Base without rest?"

And with that, Moon Man fluffed up his Moon Pillow
and began to snore, making the sound that only a
Moon Man would make while snoring.

"I can't wait for tomorrow!" said Moon Man,
as he fell fast asleep.

Just then, Buzzy was distracted by the sounds of some hearty laughter.

"Yo-Ho-Ho!" said Captain Pirate and his Pirate crew.
"Where be that thar treasure?!"

"It's buried right here, I think!" said Buzzy.

"Bring out yer shovels and yer spades, mateys!" said Captain Pirate.

"Dig! Dig!" squealed Buzzy.

"And you should rest your weary bones too, Buzzy,"
said Captain Pirate.
"For tomorrow will be a day to remember!"

And with that, Captain Pirate and his Pirate Crew
put away their shovels and spades,

stretched out across
the warm sand,

and fell fast asleep.

"We are!" said Buzzy. "Let's stomp through it right now!"

But Giant Dinosaur wasn't so sure.

"I've been stomping all day," said Giant Dinosaur, "and I think I'll need a good night's sleep before I'm able to stomp through the Great Divide."

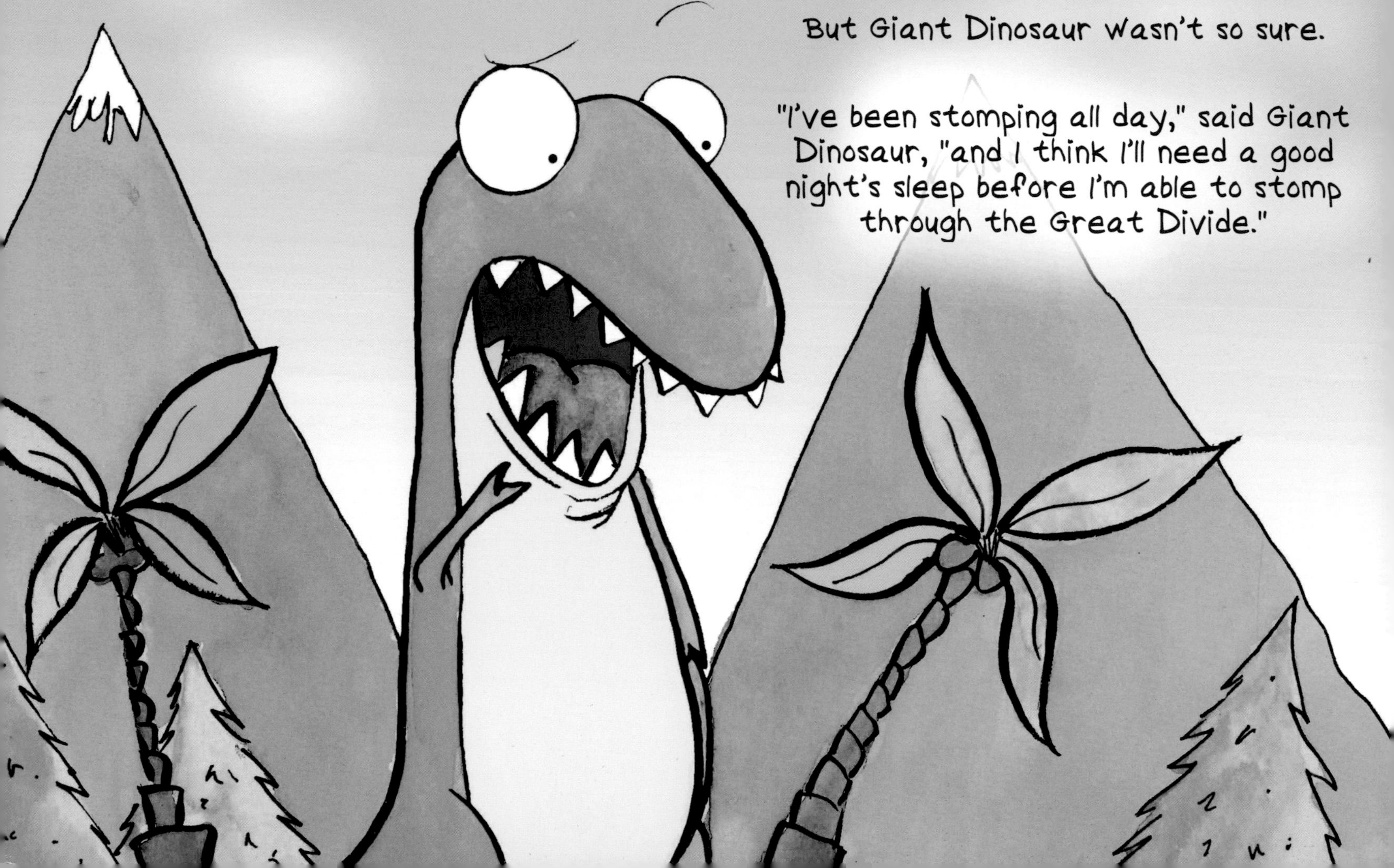

And with that, Giant Dinosaur curled up, and began to breathe heavy dinosaur breaths.

Her eyes started to slowly close.

Very soon after, she was fast asleep.

Buzzy was beginning to feel awfully sleepy. He was just about to close his eyes when he felt a poke on his side.

"Well I'll be!" exclaimed Courageous Explorer, quite courageously.
"It's the little boy who will lead us to the City of Gold!
I told you I'd find him!"

His trusty mule nodded in approval.

"Oh good!" said Buzzy. "I was afraid I'd have to go to sleep, but now I can help you find the City of Gold instead!"

"My dear Buzzy," said Courageous Explorer, "I'm afraid that won't do at all. We'll never find the City of Gold like that."

"Well, then how do we find it?" asked Buzzy.

"Don't you know?" asked Courageous Explorer.
"We must find it in your dreams!
That's the only way. We hope you'll help us!"
Courageous Explorer looked at Buzzy,
quite hopefully.

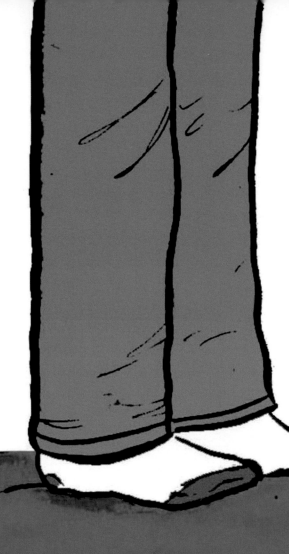

Just then, Daddy came over.
"Buzzy, it's time for bed," said Daddy.
"Are you ready?"

"I can't wait!!" proclaimed Buzzy.
And with that, Buzzy jumped right into bed.

Daddy tucked Buzzy into bed
and said goodnight.

And when Daddy turned
off the lights,
courageous Explorer
peeked out his head
just while Buzzy was
closing his eyes.

"To the City of Gold!"
whispered Courageous Explorer.

And off they went.